# Seasons

## of the

# Fuzzy

# WISHING PUFFS

## BETHANY SHERIDAN

To order additional copies of this book, contact:
Xlibris
1-888-795-4274
www.Xlibris.com
Orders@Xlibris.com

ISBN:     Softcover            978-1-7960-7436-9
          Hardcover            978-1-7960-7437-6
          EBook                978-1-7960-7435-2

Library of Congress Control Number: 2019919373

Print information available on the last page.

Rev. date: 02/20/2020

In the land of fairies, the fuzzy wishing puffs grew toward the sky.

There was still time for the fuzzy wishing puffs to be chosen by a child, a child who believed wishes were not just for birthdays.

All the fairies waited patiently for school to end each day, hoping one child would stop and pick a fuzzy wishing puff or maybe even a bouquet.

But the days turned to weeks and the April showers were due. The fairies knew nothing was ever wasted and the wishes could still be made true.

The clouds came and the sky grew darker. The season of rain had to come, without it, the flowers of May could never bloom.

The yellow fairies, with their gold hair flowing in the breeze, held tight to the stems of the fuzzy wishing puffs and to the trees.

The green fairies with their dazzling emerald eyes, stood silently in the tall grass. The blue fairies with their shimmering teal dust, looked high to the cloudy sky.

The violet fairies with their melodic voices, lifted up a prayer for each fuzzy wishing puff, knowing they would soon have to fly.

For they all knew nothing was ever wasted – the wishes could still be made, they did not have to be afraid.

The red fairies with their ruby lined wings, flew quickly through the meadow of green.

Drops began to fall and the wind pushed the fuzzy wishing puff seeds further from the land of the fairies. They watched and prayed they would make it to the next day, someone needed them in the month of May.

The fairies believed the fuzzy wishing puffs could make it through the storm. The fuzzy wishing puff seeds floated and flew whichever way the wind blew.

Some went into the forest and some to the field, some to the city and some to the car windshield.

But after the April showers had passed, the sun came again and the not so fuzzy wishing puff seeds could grow toward the sky once more. The only difference was it was now summer and with summer, came laughter.

And with laughter came adventure. And with adventure, came imagination. And with imagination, came fairies and with fairies, came fuzzy wishing puffs.

And with fuzzy wishing puffs, came hope.

The hope for today and joy for tomorrow. Because nothing is ever wasted. And for each living thing, there are seasons.

Seasons of sunshine and seasons of rain, seasons of growth and seasons of pain. But for each season, there is a fuzzy wishing puff, a prayer just for you.

One that is filled with hope and the belief that wishes and prayers do come true.

For everything there is a season, and a time for every purpose under heaven. Ecclesiastes 3:1

Printed in the United States
By Bookmasters